DO YOU EVER WONDER...

💔 Why do break-ups have to happen?

💔 Wasn't I good enough?

💔 Did I fall in love with the wrong guy?

💔 What will people think if I don't have a boyfriend?

💔 Did I expect too much?

💔 Did he expect too much?

💔 Did we have too much "togetherness"?

💔 Could we have solved our problems?

💔 Is honesty the best policy when breaking up?

💔 How do I keep going when it's over?

Find out how others have dealt with these questions ... and survived.

Other Books by
Meg Schneider

HELP! MY TEACHER HATES ME!

HELP!
MY HEART IS
BREAKING!

*How to Get Through
the Hurt*

MEG
SCHNEIDER

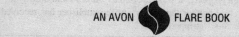

AN AVON FLARE BOOK

AVON BOOKS
A division of
The Hearst Corporation
1350 Avenue of the Americas
New York, New York 10019

First Avon Flare Printing: July 1997

AVON FLARE TRADEMARK REG. U.S. PAT. OFF. AND IN OTHER COUNTRIES,
MARCA REGISTRADA, HECHO EN U.S.A.

Printed in the U.S.A.

WCD 10 9 8 7 6 5 4 3 2 1

to GABRIELLA SUZANNE

Contents

DO YOU NEED THIS BOOK?

Chances are romantic relationships are relatively new for you. Maybe you've been trying them for a year, maybe less. Then again perhaps you've gotten a few years of boyfriends behind you. But no matter how long you've had romance in your life or even if you haven't yet started, two things are an absolute given:

ONE: You're going to experience break-ups.

TWO: You will, at least sometimes, view them as difficult and even painful events.

This is little wonder. Breaking up is a complex experience full of contradictions. It is a loss. But it is also the door to gaining thrilling new relationships. It can bring to the fore many difficult feelings, insecurities, and confusions. But it can also help you see your strengths. Break-ups reflect something sad about your relationship, but most often say nothing about the core of your relationship.

Here is a critical thought to keep in mind as you consider this book. We will return to it throughout:

Break-ups are not the mark of an unsuccessful

relationship. They simply mark the end of one relationship.

Break-ups can be tough, but they should not be allowed to achieve so much importance as to overwhelm in your heart and mind the experience of the relationship.

Of course understanding this fact, and letting it help you cope with a break-up are two different things entirely. Hopefully by the end of this book you will be able to fit everything together. But right now, since you picked up this book, chances are you need a little help understanding how to handle the end of a romance . . .

YOU NEED THIS BOOK IF
AFTER YOUR BOYFRIEND BREAKS UP WITH YOU:

- You feel put down.
- You are convinced you did something wrong.
- You are unable to speak. Only cry. You can't discuss a thing with him.
- You're convinced if you'd only been prettier, smarter, or. . . .
- You don't want to risk caring about someone again.
- You want your boyfriend back even though you know the relationship really wasn't a good one.
- You keep finding yourself trying to win your ex back.

- Your boyfriend confesses he's gotten involved with someone else.
- You feel like you'll never get over your last boyfriend.
- You're worried that everyone you know thinks you're a loser.
- You keep worrying that your new boyfriend is going to break up with you too.

OR IF YOU'RE THE ONE WHO WANTS TO BREAK UP:

- You can't figure out what to say.
- You're afraid he's going to be extremely upset.
- He begs you to give it one more try and you feel torn.
- He begs you to give it one more try and you feel guilty.
- He won't stop pursuing you.
- Yet you don't because you're afraid of being alone.

There is no easy way to break up. But there are positive and negative ways.

Breaking up constructively, meaning with care and sensitivity and in a way that helps both parties feel respected and not belittled, is a skill. A necessary skill. If you're going to become involved and share intimate thoughts and feelings, then you owe it to yourself and your partner to at least attempt a caring break-up when it's time to say good-bye. (The word "attempt" is used because you can't be caring alone. He has to try too!)

Breaking up never gets easier, but definitely can become less frightening and overwhelming once you understand the *real* reasons break-ups occur and how to maneuver yourself through the closing moments. You need to understand why they happen, what they mean (and don't mean), and finally the mechanics of how to do it no matter where you stand on the matter.

This book will help. Nothing can replace experience of course, and neither this book, nor any number of break-ups will be able to stop the hurt.

But with good skills, understanding, and experience you will gain a perspective that will honor the last relationship, and see you confidently through to the next romance . . . and then the next . . . and the next. Because, after all, once a relationship is over, and you've recovered, what matters most is what's to come!

ONE

WHY DO BREAK-UPS HAVE TO HAPPEN?

No one likes to break up. No matter who is doing the breaking up there is pain on both sides. And even if both people think it's the right thing to do, it can hurt in a very bittersweet way.

There are bitter feelings because pulling away from someone with whom you have been close can feel very harsh. It is sweet because of the tenderness you can remember feeling and because of everything that you know is to come with someone new.

Which brings us to the reason why break-ups happen.

Break-ups have to happen, quite simply, because you are growing and changing. Past loves no longer seem to "fit," while new loves seem to promise something "more." Breaking up is a necessary opportunity to learn more about who you are, what you need, and who you can be.

It is also a necessary loss, which is why it hurts.

Unfortunately, we all grew up believing in the basic message of fairy tales. One day Prince Charming would come along, and whisk us away without a glance backward.

Snow White, if you notice, didn't date. Neither did Cinderella. They didn't eye different guys, and they weren't rejected by their love interests. Nor, when they got together with their princes, did we read about misunderstandings between them, or moments when they wondered if they had indeed chosen the right partner—or anything else that we living, breathing, feeling people do!

They just met, after doing a lot of sleeping and cleaning, fell in love, and that was that.

It's little wonder that when romance first enters our lives we get swept away by the joy of it, and caught off balance by the pain!

But the truth is, break-ups, when you are young, are natural stepping stones to new experiences which in turn help you grow and learn about yourself, and other people.

WHY CAN'T I JUST GROW AND CHANGE WITH THE SAME PERSON?

Sometimes you can. Older, more experienced people can grow together. Many happily married people report that they were able to grow and change with each other. Usually this means as each person began to have new interests, or grew more serious or developed a change in values, the other partner was able to comfortably adapt to these changes. And vice versa.

But there's a difference between these older persons and you. By the time they got married, they already had learned quite a bit about themselves. They'd met all kinds of people and had had an assortment of girlfriends and boyfriends who taught them what kind of traits they needed in a partner. They'd learned basically what sort of person they would be most happy with, because they'd also grown to know themselves better.

But you are not there yet. You still have a lot to learn about what you want out of life and from the person with whom you connect. Do you need someone super confident and aggressive? Or are you more comfortable with a less confident, very sensitive sort of boy? Is brains the most important thing to you, or will you discover a good sense of humor is critical? Are you turned on by a very active sports type because you enjoy that too, or do you want a quiet intellectual? Then there is the vast unknown. Sometimes what we think we want in a person is not nearly as important as qualities we discover we need only when they're missing!

Also, you need time to develop interpersonal skills and a sense of self that will enable you to have a healthy relationship.

YOU HAVE TO LEARN TO LOVE

Feeling as if you love a person is not enough to keep it going. You also need to learn how to be a supportive and loving partner to someone else. And you need a chance to develop a firm sense of your own strengths so that you can function as an independent person in the relationship. This is something that usually comes after a person has experience with romance.

At first the tendency might be to lose yourself in someone. What he likes, you like. What he pursues, so do you. His friends become yours. Or yours his.

After a while, however, you might begin to see the down side of such an intense connection. Ironically, despite all that closeness you may feel lost. As if you don't know your own self anymore. You will experience the need to keep something that is all your own. And by actually doing so, you will discover that keeping your personal boundaries intact can make for a terrific romance.

There are other common mistakes you might make. Perhaps you expect too much from a boyfriend? Or maybe too little? Maybe what you're most attracted to isn't really good for you. (You may like super go-getters, but perhaps you end up feeling overwhelmed by their constant need to go and do.) Perhaps you're in love with love, and tend not to even "see" the person you're with.

None of this makes you a bad person. It just makes you one who has to grow into her ability to truly love.

THE DESIRE TO EXPERIMENT

And then there is simply the fact that this is a time to experiment. Not only do you *need* to try out new relationships in order to learn about yourself, other people, and the world, but many kids experience this as a *drive* to do so.

You might think, "Peter is funny and lovely to kiss, but James is cute too. I wonder what it would be like to be with him. I wonder if he'd like me? It's been romantic being with Peter, but James has been flirting with me and he's *so* cute . . ."

In other words it's not only something you *have* to do, it's something you may *want* to do.

It's not that your affection for a person, or some-one's for you, isn't real—it is. But deep involve-ments, at this time, will often not work in the face of a desire to explore.

WHY DOES HE WANT TO SEE
WHAT "IT'S" LIKE WITH OTHER GIRLS?
WHY DO I WONDER ABOUT OTHER BOYS?

Love is exciting. Feeling physically attracted to someone brings with it all sorts of wonderful sensations. Wanting to try out being emotionally or physically close with someone new is all part of growing up.

Consider this. Your body is changing now, and probably clothes you always admired which weren't quite right for your figure, now fit in a flattering way. So you buy a great dress and you feel wonderful in it. But now it's been a month or so and you're wandering through a store and see several other dresses that you think would look great too. You still love the dress you have, but the idea of having something new, some-thing in a slightly different style seems so excit-ing. "I wonder what I'd look like in that," you think, imagining the pleasures of finally being able to wear something so "mature" with ease.

Well, deciding that one wants to look further in the field of romance is much like that. Of course the big difference is that you can't hang a person up in a closet and get back to him later if you feel like it. Dresses don't have feelings. People can't be treated like objects.

And so break-ups occur.

Certainly you can try to have it all. You can

say to a boyfriend or he can say to you, "I still like you very much, but I feel like I need to date other people. Can we still go out sometimes but not be each other's only anymore?"

Sometimes, if both people are feeling mutually "itchy" for something new, this can work. But most times it can't. Most times when it comes to ending a relationship, two people are in different places.

And that's where the real pain comes in.

No one likes to be left, and no one likes to hurt a person they were once close to. Of course the former pain is more heartbreaking. It would have to be. Yearning for someone who no longer wants to be with you can be terribly distressing.

But there's another reason that it can hurt a lot, which many people experience and which is totally misguided.

WASN'T I GOOD ENOUGH?

The simple answer is *yes* you probably were.

The complicated answer is, it usually has nothing to do with that (or you) at all.

When it comes to love, relationships don't just last by virtue of how worthy one person is of the other's adoration. This is because the ability of one person to experience deep feelings for another is profoundly affected by timing, age, emotional strengths and weaknesses, and very personal (and often temporary and highly variable) likes and dislikes.

The problem is, the person being rejected often gets lost in a swamp of insecurity. "If only I'd been prettier. Or smarter. Or more interesting. If only I hadn't said this or that. If only my teeth were straighter, my legs longer, my humor better, my laugh brighter."

And yet all the while, none of this had much to do with the break-up at all. Certainly you aren't perfect. Nobody is. When you feel drawn to a person the imperfections don't matter. And it's true that when you get ready to pull away, you may allow the imperfections to become more visible so that it's easier to break up.

But, and this is key, the "getting ready to pull away" part usually has much more to do with the person pulling away than the person who is being left. If some boy breaks up with you it is *not* a simple case of him deciding you're not as good as he thought you were.

Jessica was devastated. Two months ago, Philip had thought she was the greatest. But suddenly two weeks ago he informed her that he wasn't feeling the same way anymore. In fact, and he said this gently, he'd met someone else he was interested in and he wanted her to hear it from him and not from someone else. Jessica had nodded as if she understood. These things happen.

But the only thing she had understood was that somehow she hadn't withstood the test of time. Philip, she was sure, had gotten a look at everything that was wrong with her and decided she simply didn't have what it took to keep him.

Jessica could not stop crying. Could not stop looking at herself critically in the mirror or thinking everything she said was stupid.

Until yesterday. It was, she thought with a sad smile, unbelievable.

Philip, it seemed, had broken up with his new girlfriend. Rumor had it he'd told her he wanted to operate independently for a while. The poor girl was seen crying on the back steps of the school.

Jessica began to understand.

Suddenly her reflection in the mirror seemed so much more appealing. . . .

●━━━━━━━━━━━━━━━━━━━●

It is a complex combination of factors that makes a person ready to move on.

This issue will be explored in more detail later on in this book, but for now, do try and keep the following in mind when it comes to break-ups.

They are, for you, the natural course of events. They are not a reflection of how good or bad you are, but rather *where* you are in life.

Surely you know by now that life is not always a picnic.

Well, love isn't either. It's just that sometimes it can feel so wonderful, that it's hard to tolerate the loss.

You can, however, get through it.

And you can also minimize the frequency of painful, difficult break-ups.

You start by choosing the right boy for all the right reasons.

TWO

HOW TO AVOID
UNNECESSARY BREAK-UPS

Given that breaking up can be so hurtful, you will want to go through one as infrequently as possible. While it is true most break-ups happen because of the urge to experience new relationships and the simple fact that you and your partners are constantly changing, there are other reasons at work in the background. As a result of these reasons, break-ups can become even more likely and more painful. The bad news is, the reasons are common.

The good news is, you can control them.

Reason One: You are choosing the wrong guy. You are selecting boys with whom you are destined for trouble.

Reason Two: you have a number of faulty ideas about what a boy can do for you and so you hasten the demise of the relationship. Expecting unreal things from a real person never works.

Break-ups, in other words, can be in the cards before either one of you ever says, "He/She's for me."

Your boyfriend may not have been right for you in the first place. In other words, the day you started seeing each other, you were already miles apart!

The thing is it didn't clearly feel that way. Sure, you might have felt a little tension when he didn't get your jokes, or understand your problems. And yes, you might have noticed he flirted a little too obviously with your friend. But still, you thought he was just what you wanted.

Ignoring the signals that someone may not be right for you doesn't make you a foolish person. It's quite common for one person to be attracted to another despite the fact that the "fit" may not be quite right. Perhaps he's super smart and you love the way he speaks, or you think he's wonderfully handsome or you're turned on by the fact that he's the best basketball player on the team and he's got a beautiful smile.

You can't help who you're attracted to.

But you can help how invested you become in him.

You don't have to say to yourself, "I'd like to have a 'thing' with him even though he's a little aggressive for me." Instead you can say, "I'm attracted to him. He's probably not the right guy but it would be fun to hang with him every once in a while."

The other thing you can help is noticing the sort of person with whom you'd be happiest. What traits do you really enjoy in a boy? What kinds of personalities do you respond to with your best self? Or to put it another way, with what sort of person do you feel the strongest connection?

Part of what makes a person fall for another cannot be easily defined. There is definitely something chemical or "magical" about an attraction. But what makes a relationship work does not reside so much in this enchanted realm. A happy relationship (even if it ends in a breakup) works because the people involved pay attention to what they need to feel lovingly connected.

Many people, however, move too quickly into a romance for all the wrong reasons. In so doing, they set themselves up for very unnecessary break-ups. These you want to avoid. And the best way to do it is to know what you're doing and feeling when you are with a boy.

SO WHY DID YOU CHOOSE HIM?

There is nothing bad about going out with a guy you are attracted to who is not quite right for a steady thing. If you don't count on him for too much you won't get hurt.

The problems begin when you ignore this and you start getting heavily involved. Doing so is very unwise and potentially disastrous. Even when in love you need to think with your head and not just your heart. There is never any percentage in trying to fool yourself into thinking things will work out. Or that the reason you like him is something other than what it is. You will only be setting the stage for a very painful ending.

Consider the list of common ill-fated reasons many people choose the "wrong guy."

- He's gorgeous.

- He's extremely popular and everyone will admire you.

- He seems to think you're great and you love the attention.

- He's exciting and a little unpredictable. "Landing" him will be a real triumph.

- Someone else has just broken up with you and the new guy's so adoring.

- You don't think you're that attractive, and he likes you, so you'd better jump at the chance.

- He's an amazing flirt and you're not sure you can trust him, but when he showers attention on you it makes you feel special.

These are only some of the reasons that you might choose the wrong partner. Generally speaking, if you choose a guy because you simply want a boyfriend, or because you feel insecure and need to prove something, you could be setting yourself up for a very unsatisfying and insecure relationship, not to mention a very painful break-up.

Relationships that begin with the wrong guy can feel as intense as ones that begin with the right one. Perhaps even more so, because as the evidence that things are not right mounts, the desire to cling to him can grow extraordinarily powerful.

Which is too bad. It was never him you loved. It was the *idea* of him. The idea which somehow made you think, "This is love." It's hard to let go of that fantasy.

And, when the break-up finally happens it can be devastating.

THE RIGHT GUY, THE WRONG REASONS

There is also the possibility that you could choose the right guy, but for the wrong reasons! Many girls harbor misguided ideas about what a relationship or a boy can do. Boys are not like heroes on TV. They aren't always strong. They can't always save you. Nor do they often have the money to buy flowers and candy and other tokens of affection. He may not kiss the way you like it right away, and he may feel shy just when you want him to act assertive. Also, a boyfriend can't make other problems in your life disappear simply by his existence.

And he certainly can't make your romance be storybook. No real romance ever is. We'll talk about this some more in the next chapter, but for now, keep this in mind. If you want a boyfriend because you want a wonderful, romantic, beautiful, magical love in your life, you'd be better off buying a romance novel or renting a romantic movie. This is not to say that you won't have your true and gloriously loving moments with a boy. But real life is such that all relationships have some problems. And if you expect that a romance is going to fix everything, or that it will be nothing but soft words, gentle hugs, endless understanding, and sweet kisses, you are bound for a big disappointment.

SO HOW DO I STOP MYSELF FROM STARTING A ROMANCE THAT SHOULDN'T BE?

By being as honest with yourself as you possibly can.

And by recognizing the faulty thinking behind some of the reasons you might want a boyfriend. There is nothing wrong with having the thoughts and feelings. It's just that acting upon them can bring very unfortunate results. Facing the truth about why you want a guy can help keep you from making poor decisions. Those "ill-fated" reasons people choose each other can be avoided when things are seen in a clear honest light:

I DON'T WANT TO BE ALONE. Loneliness is a painful feeling. But being around someone with whom you are not truly connecting can be even worse. Besides, are you really alone? Probably you have friends. Of course you may have a dismal Saturday night on your own, but that doesn't mean you are all alone. It just means that you are on your own, more than you'd like.

I'M AFRAID OF WHAT OTHERS WILL THINK IF I DON'T HAVE A GUY. Do you really want to stir up your feelings of attachment, so that others will notice you can get a guy? Do you really want to waste time with someone who isn't right for you so that you can proudly say, "My boyfriend's name is . . . ?" And what will these "others" think after you've been clinging to this relationship and he breaks up with you? If the relationship is a lie, it won't last. You're going to have to face what others think sooner or later. Better to be forever independent than regularly dumped. And this is so for your own self-image. Mid morning gossip sessions shouldn't matter.

I'VE GOTTA GET ANOTHER GUY SO I DON'T LOOK FOOLISH!
But everyone goes through break-ups! Yes, you may worry that people are thinking, "Poor Lisa. She got dumped," but consider what their very next thought will probably be. "Boy, I hope that doesn't happen to me," is a good bet. And if someone does start passing hurtful rumors about you such as, "Lisa can't keep a guy," know one thing. Only a person who is afraid this is true of herself would say it about you.

IF I HAVE A BOYFRIEND, I KNOW I'M WORTH SOMETHING.
If you are completely dependent on someone else to make you feel good about yourself, you are going to be hurt a lot. In order to be able to stand up for yourself in a relationship and choose the boy who is right for you at any given time, you have to believe that you deserve to be treated well, and to select someone who "fits." If you do not feel good about yourself on your own, you will tolerate mistreatment and settle for the wrong guy, simply because you don't feel you can do better. What a horrible way to treat yourself!

•━━━━━━━━━━━━━•

Laurie had never felt more powerful. More sure of herself. She and Steve had been "an item" and it was, she thought, proof positive of her good looks and attractive personality. Certainly there had been days when, before Steve entered her life, she'd felt good about herself. But it wasn't consistent.

When Steve entered the picture, she began waking up every morning feeling like a star.

Until, that is, she got the call from Steve.

The call that it was over. Surely, he said, she had sensed things were cooling off. But Laurie insisted she hadn't. Secretly she'd intuited a certain distance between them, but she'd pushed the feeling away. Having a "boyfriend" was just too important for her to worry about the details.

"Can't we just try and make it work?" Laurie asked tearfully. Her eyes traveled to her reflection in the mirror. She wasn't looking good today, she thought. Maybe this is how she actually looked every day. No wonder Steve didn't want her anymore.

"I know we can work it out," Laurie continued, desperately trying to fight off the feeling that she was, once again, not much at all.

But Steve remained firm, and Laurie hung up feeling like a damp mop.

❧━━━━━━━━━━━━━━━━━━━━━❧

IF I GO OUT WITH A REAL HUNK, EVERYONE WILL THINK I'M SPECIAL. Not necessarily. Sure, they may think, "Wow, she must be really great," but then what happens when you break up? And wouldn't you rather have someone think you're special because *you've* got a great sense of humor, or *you're* really smart and understanding? It's very nice to be admired. But only when it's for who you are, and not what you can do, or who you can "get."

<u>I HATE MY FAMILY, MY FRIENDS NEVER STICK, BUT A BOY-FRIEND WILL HELP.</u> If you're having trouble with your family, or trouble making friends, then you are having trouble with your family and making friends. You have to resolve those problems. A boyfriend won't help. He may be an arm to lean on. But that responsibility might also scare him away. A boyfriend would simply be a Band-Aid, something you put over a wound. He won't fix it. *You* need to address your problems directly and then your boyfriend can be what he should be. A boy should be someone with whom you feel close, and not your escape hatch or life line. That's too big a job for him. He still has a life of his own that he needs to manage.

<u>IT DOESN'T REALLY MATTER HOW HE TREATS ME. I KNOW HE CARES. WE HAVE SOMETHING SPECIAL.</u> Anytime you find yourself falling into this way of thinking, you can bet you are not involved with a boy for the right reason. There is no acceptable reason for anyone to treat you poorly. The only reason that you might accept such negative behaviors is because you are too afraid not to. Maybe you think you aren't good enough to expect more. Maybe you'd just do anything to be attached to someone. But whatever the reason, if you start making excuses for a boyfriend who treats you insensitively or cruelly, then you definitely have a boyfriend for the wrong reasons.

Finally, there's one other reason why it's a bad idea to want a boyfriend for the wrong reasons. And that's the boy.

Suppose you decide you have to have a boyfriend for any of the above-mentioned reasons. You don't *really* care for him, and then some other guy comes along. What do you do then? Just break up with the one you're with and waltz off with the new boy? What if the guy you've been dating has strong feelings about you? Again, even if you aren't right for each other, one or both of you could still grow seriously attached.

You could end up hurting him for no good reason. You could end up doing something to someone that you wouldn't want done to you, and all because you were too afraid to stand on your own and wait for the right person.

Choosing a boy for the wrong reasons can end up hurting both people very much. A relationship built on very little substance can only cause unnecessary pain, not just at the end, but during too. Yes, break-ups between people who have enjoyed a healthy relationship are painful. But at least you will both know you had your time together and it was wonderful.

If you've got to go through a break-up, wouldn't you rather know it was worth it?

FINALLY, THE *GOOD* REASONS

Now that you know the "wrong" reasons for choosing a boy and getting involved, let's take a look at what some solid, healthy reasons might be.

- You genuinely like him and he likes you.
- It feels good spending time together.
- When you're with each other you feel appreciated.
- You enjoy doing many of the same things.
- You understand most of each other's thoughts and feelings.
- You are able to talk about happy and painful things concerning life, each other, and your relationship.
- You are learning something about what it means to care about someone and to be there for him.

Having a boyfriend because you feel good together makes for the healthiest relationship. It will usually not result in a break-up every other month. Relationships born of desperation are a lot rockier and end a lot quicker and nastier (in most cases) than those born of true affection. When and if the time comes to part, it will hurt, even if you both agree it's time to move on. But you will have had the experience of a healthy, warm relationship in which you both felt loved and admired. You will realize it will happen again.

You will not feel nearly as defeated as you will feel enriched by the happy times in the relationship.

THREE

KEEPING LOVE ALIVE—
STAYING REASONABLE IN ROMANCE

A romance cannot feel wonderful all of the time.

You are two different people with different needs and interests and desires and problems and sometimes you will simply be "in a different place." He has an upsetting fight with a friend and so he only listens to you with half an ear and you feel ignored. You're busy thinking about your upcoming tennis match and so you miss his joke. One of you feels like spending a Sunday afternoon alone. The other wants to hang out together in the park. You misunderstand each other and so end up in a fight over something very little, or nothing at all.

None of this means you should break up.

It just means you're having a real relationship.

A real relationship much like others in your life. You might squabble with your sister or brother over renting a movie. Yet later that evening you might share a joke that leaves you feeling very close to each other. You and your best friend might have a falling-out over a game of tennis, but days later consider the issue *very* unimportant. Relationships have their wonderful and difficult moments.

The problem is a lot of people don't realize this goes for romance as well.

Their expectations of each other and the way the romance should feel are too high. And that's what brings on the break-up.

It's not the less-than-perfect moment that causes the problem.

It's their reaction to it.

Break-ups are going to happen. But why make them happen if the cause is something you can control?

UNREASONABLE EXPECTATIONS

Life, as stated earlier, is not a fairy tale. Nor is it like the movies. Not every boy is super romantic. You're not always beautiful or witty and warm. No one is patient, funny, exciting to be with, great to talk to, or even very thoughtful all of the time. You can't be and he can't be.

It's important to take a closer look at the unfair expectations you may place on your partner. The ones which could end up in an untimely break-up. (Certainly boys can have unfair expectations of girls as well, but I am not addressing them right now. You cannot control a boy's behavior. Only your own.) By knowing what these expectations are, and understanding why they are asking too much, you might very well avoid a difficult break-up and actually even improve your relationship!

Lisa's week at school had been awful. She nearly failed the history test and her best friend was angry that twice she hadn't saved her a seat at the lunch table. Lisa couldn't wait for Saturday night and a chance to be with her boyfriend Matt. In fact she was just settling down to call him and make a plan when the phone rang. It was Matt, beside himself with excitement because he'd been handed a ticket to a big basketball game for that Saturday night.

Lisa promptly began to catalog her woes, winding up with, "So you see, I . . . I . . . need you," sputtered with disbelief.

"Well, we could spend some time together Saturday afternoon!" Matt responded immediately.

"I can't then," Lisa snapped. "I can't believe a basketball game is more important than me!"

"It's not that it's more important . . ." Matt struggled to find a way to say this nicely. "It's just that this never happens. I don't get handed a ticket to a big game like this every day. I have to go. I just have to . . ."

"So go," Lisa said coldly. And then she hung up.

They didn't speak again until Sunday. Lisa couldn't wait anymore for Matt to call, and so she called him.

He did not sound particularly happy to hear from her.

This upset her a lot. She'd figured the whole thing would have blown over.

Insisting that to have a truly good romance, you must always be the most important thing in your boyfriend's life, is unfair. Sometimes other issues in his life will take precedence. Not allowing for this fact is a very quick road to break-up city.

EXPECTING HIM TO KNOW
WITHOUT YOU HAVING TO SAY

Boyfriends are not mind readers. Sometimes people think that if they are really in sync with another person, they will hardly have to speak. Each person will automatically know how the other is feeling. A wonderful romance means you completely understand each other.

But this isn't so. A wonderful romance is one in which you each want to try to understand each other. But that's it.

It is unreasonable to expect that when your boyfriend teases you about something, he knows he's hurting you. Of course if he repeatedly pokes fun at something you've already told him is upsetting to you, that's a different story. But having to say to your boyfriend upon his first tease, "You know actually I'm sensitive about my freckles. Please don't tease me about that," is part of helping someone get to know you. It's an indication, in fact, of trust. You are revealing a vulnerability to someone and trusting he will understand. *That* is the sign of a lovely romance.

CONSTANT TOGETHERNESS

People need space. They need to pursue their own interests. They need to just be by themselves and think. They need to fulfill their responsibility to the many people in their lives. And they need to develop a sense of independence and the confidence that they can stand on their own.

You may love being with your boyfriend. The two of you may want to spend a lot of time together. But it is a mistake to ask for constant togetherness. While you are important people in each other's lives, room has to be made for others. You may need to be there for a friend. He may need to help his sister. You may want to watch a skating exhibition. He may prefer to go to a soccer game. These things have to be respected. To attempt to deny the differences between you, or the fact that there are other people that matter in your lives, is to ignore the truth.

It will also leave each of you way too vulnerable to each other. Way too afraid of being deserted. The more you spend time only with each other, the more dependent you will become and the more other people will resentfully drop away. You may not feel you need them in the good times, but what about the bad? Who will you turn to then?

The ultimate result is that each of you could lose your ability to stand up for yourselves. You could become too afraid that an argument will end in a break-up. You could be left with a relationship that rests on secret resentments and exists only for fear of it not existing at all.

WANTING HIM TO FIT A MOLD

Your boyfriend can only be who he is. Certainly you can try to sway him a little in one direction or another. You might want to help him open up more about his feelings, or inspire him to enjoy a romantic moment or encourage him to laugh more.

But you can't change the essentials of who he is. You can't turn a loner into a social animal. You can't make an unathletic person into the star of the team. And you can't turn a flirt who likes to eye every girl who passes by into a solidly committed "one-girl-for-me" kind of guy.

Trying to do so is unfair to both of you.

Which is why it's always important not to leap into a relationship too quickly, and also why the, "I'll change him once I get him" syndrome is so misguided.

You can't change a person unless he wants to change and unless he *can* change. People are not born blank slates. Some things they just simply are. The surest way to a break-up is to plunge into a relationship with a guy who isn't quite right, thinking "We'll work out the knots later."

If you sense there's a mismatch between you, try some casual time together to see if it melts away. If it doesn't, moving into a more intimate relationship could be a big mistake. It won't bring you closer. It will only make you feel trapped with the wrong guy and vice versa.

The only place to go from there is down and out.

REALISTIC EXPECTATIONS

Unrealistic expectations can easily ruin a relationship.

On the other hand, *not* expecting certain things in a relationship can also make for a very unhappy experience. You have a right to expect particular behaviors and "treatment" from your boyfriend. Break-ups are terribly upsetting, but being treated badly is worse.

Know your romantic rights! It's the best way to make sure you get them.

HONESTY

You have the right to expect that your boyfriend will be honest with you. That he will not hide other relationships or say things that aren't true or talk you into doing things by playing on your insecurities. You may not need to break up with the first deception. But a pattern simply won't do.

●━━━━━━━━━━━━━━━━━━━━━━━━━━●

Jessie had been in love with Andy from afar all year. When he finally asked her out, she could not believe her good fortune.

She'd always been insecure and when they turned into a couple it felt as if it were happening to another person. Everyone knew they were seeing each other. She was finally a somebody.

But soon after they became known as a unit, Jessie started feeling unsure. Scared. Certain she was about to lose him. For one thing, she knew there were rumors that he was chasing another girl. When she asked him he insisted it wasn't true.

"You're beautiful," he'd claimed. "I care about you a lot. I wouldn't go after anyone else."

She didn't quite believe him, but still hoped that this one flirtation would simply blow over.

Besides, Andy kissed her a lot. Jessie only sort

of liked that though. It somehow didn't always feel
warm. Or real.

But Jessie said nothing. In fact, every time she
felt uncomfortable or upset, she'd push it aside.

About a month later Andy suddenly an-
nounced he was sorry, but things had changed.
He was taking Michelle to the dance.

This, just three days after he'd assured her that
she was the best thing in ninth grade.

———————————•———————————

You can never have a loving relationship with
someone you can't trust. The truth may cause
problems. You may even break up because of it.
But lies will almost always eventually result in a
break-up, along with terrible feelings of betrayal.

That is an extra pain you don't need.

BASIC RESPECT

You have a right to expect your boyfriend will
accord you behaviors that in effect say, "You deserve to be treated nicely and with concern for
and interest in your thoughts and feelings." This
means, among other things:

- He should speak to you in a manner that
  indicates you count. Even when he is angry, his manner should show he under-
  stands you are a person and not a "verbal
  punching bag."

- He shouldn't tease you in public or private
  in a way that might hurt your feelings.

- He shouldn't criticize you in public or cruelly in private.

- When you are making a point, he should hear you out instead of interrupting and insisting on his opinion.

- He should behave in a way that makes it clear he does not believe your life should revolve around his.

- He should never, under any circumstances, push, shove, or hit you. Physical abuse is not acceptable even if he has every reason to be angry. We will discuss this in detail later in the book.

You deserve to be treated like a separate person. Someone who does not exist just for your boyfriend, and who has a right to thoughts, feelings, and ideas that may differ from his.

SENSITIVITY

You have a right to expect your feelings to be considered. While, as discussed earlier, you cannot expect your boyfriend to always know how you will react, once you tell him you have a right to expect he will remember. If you are sensitive about your thin hair, or your poor performance at school, or your father's drinking, he has no right to talk of these issues in a way that either makes light of them or sounds critical . . . even if he says in the face of your hurt, "I'm just being honest."

He isn't just being that. Honesty is some people's excuse for insensitivity. You have the right to expect better, that he will listen and change his behavior. You have a right to expect your boyfriend to help you with your areas of vulnerability, and not make them worse.

GENEROSITY OF SPIRIT

You have a right to expect your boyfriend to behave in a giving way toward you. This means he will ask you what's bothering you when your voice sounds funny. He will do nice things for you when you're not feeling well, such as make you a card, or bring you a little present, or simply make an extra effort to visit. When you're very upset about something and you snap at him, he will understand and not get angry. (Though he should expect you to apologize.)

You cannot always be a giving person. Sometimes you will be sad or angry or irritable. You have a right to expect that your boyfriend can accept this and reach out. (And of course he has the right to the same from you when it is his turn to be impossible!)

Finally, in order to keep love healthy and alive, one other component is particularly necessary. You should expect to like yourself.

YOU NEED TO LIKE YOURSELF IN YOUR ROMANCE

It's as important for you to like yourself in a romance as it is for you to like your boyfriend. You will need to be your own very good friend and admirer because there will be times in a relationship when you have to stand up for yourself, have to be sure, have to know what you want or need.

You can't do that if you don't much like what's happening to you in the relationship. If you're feeling beaten down, or frightened, it will be quite difficult to make sure your needs are met. You should expect more from yourself than that.

The best way to feel good about yourself in a

romance is to feel confident about the way you are behaving in it. Because then if you get into an argument you will not be swayed into pretending you believe something you don't. And if you actually break up, you will keep the painful second-guesses to a minimum. You won't have to drive yourself crazy with such thoughts as.

- Maybe I was too demanding.
- If I'd only been nicer.
- Does it really matter that he lies? I know he likes me.
- So what if he likes to make jokes about me. Maybe I was just too sensitive.

And you also won't find yourself behaving in ways that you think will make him happy, even though it doesn't feel right to you.

- You won't hang out with his friends if you think they're a bit too wild. You'll be able to say, "You go. They make me uncomfortable."
- You won't agree with everything he says, when you don't. You'll be able to say you feel differently about things without fear of him walking away.
- You won't give in to his requests for physical intimacy, no matter what they are, if it feels wrong to you. You will remain firm in your knowledge that physical closeness is an expression of emotional closeness. It should never be a tool to "keep" someone.

You *will not*, in other words, feel the need to save the romance, *at all costs*.

If you can feel confident about the way you behaved in a relationship, then when it ends, for whatever reason, you will feel okay. Strong even.

There are some things you just can't control. You can't control his feelings, his demands, his behaviors, or his desires.

The only thing you can control is you.

But that's a big thing, and in fact it's the thing that counts the most in a break-up. If you can believe in yourself, if you can trust that you behaved in a way that was correct and good for you during the relationship, then even if you're hurt you will cope more easily with the loss.

FOUR

WHEN THE TROUBLE DOESN'T GO AWAY

Difficult or upsetting times occur in every relationship.

But what of the rough times that don't go away?

What about when the problems seem to crop up frequently and with a fair amount of intensity?

Does this mean it's time to consider a breakup?

Not necessarily.

It could mean you two aren't communicating very well and that it's time to see if there's enough interest in each other to work on improving the relationship.

HOW TO KNOW IF IT'S WORTH A LITTLE WORK

It's never a great idea to run the moment the going gets tough. Too many questions get left unanswered. Too many "What ifs . . ." or "If onlys . . ." can haunt you. "What if I'd talked about how angry I was instead of hanging up the phone? If only I hadn't just told him off. What if he was telling me the truth and he didn't ask someone else out? If only I hadn't flirted with James behind his back."

Lots of times it feels easier not to struggle through a problem. It's scary to talk about things that could hurt and to reveal things about yourself you'd rather not think about or discuss. It is difficult to admit to your own mistakes and to be mature enough to accept others'-faults.

It takes strength. Patience. Stick-to-itiveness.

It also takes liking a person enough to put in the "work."

Allowing your pride, or impatience, or sensitivity to keep you from trying to sort out your differences would be a big and painful mistake.

Of course one reason you may choose not to work on things is that in your heart you don't much care about the person. You might simply want to step away. Sometimes two people just aren't a good match. That's fine.

But if you do care, remember that enduring problems doesn't mean you are all wrong for each other. They may mean that you need to communicate better. To put a little more effort into the relationship.

It can take strength, courage, and patience, but the results can be well worth the venture.

HOW TO BEGIN RESOLVING YOUR PROBLEMS

The best way to sort out a relationship problem is through a three-step approach. For each step it's important not to rush, to be as honest with yourself as possible, and to be accountable for what you say and do. This means putting action behind your words.

STEP 1. Openly talk about your problems.

STEP 2. Decide what actions each of you will take to correct things.

STEP 3. Follow through on your actions and wait a reasonable amount of time to see if things between you improve.

This stage of the relationship is going to feel a little like an experiment. Can you make it work, or not? There's no point fretting too much about it. Things will either "click" or they won't. This is your best shot. Here'a detailed look at how to use these steps to their best advantage.

Note: You will need the cooperation of your boyfriend throughout this process. What happens is not entirely up to you. Hopefully he will take the steps with you. If not, consider it a further indication that the relationship may not work.

OPENLY TALK ABOUT YOUR PROBLEM. Tell your boyfriend the next time the tension hits that you think the two of you need to talk. Then lead with something positive, so that he knows you are not on the attack and that you care about him very much. Take it slow. He will need time to get with the program.

"I really like you but I feel as if we are upsetting each other a lot. I keep trying to figure out why we seem to make each other feel bad. I have some ideas about it and I was wondering if you'd like to talk about it."

Your boyfriend may shrug, or say "Not really," or he may be relieved that the two of you are going to bring things out into the open. If he is pleased, then you can launch right into what you're thinking. If he isn't, try saying something like, "I do need to talk. I think if we shared what we felt inside we'd understand each other better." Expressing yourself in this way will underline the fact that you want to make things work. You will be sharing some responsibility for the problem and its correction. Doing so will create an atmosphere in which your boyfriend can more easily face his own troublesome behaviors.

Now it's time to say what's bothering you. Be as straight as you can about it. You've come this far. There's no point pretending the truth is anything other than what it is.

"I know you like to flirt with other girls. I guess you think it's fun. But even though I smile when you do it, it hurts me. Then I get very tense afterwards and we end up in a fight."

Your boyfriend might understand right away or try to minimize what you are saying. "Oh, I don't flirt that much," he might say, or, "You shouldn't get upset. It doesn't mean anything."

Remember you have a right to your feelings. No one can tell you how to feel. Your boyfriend might be saying these things because he's embarrassed or because he believes them. It doesn't really matter. You still have a right to say, "That is how I feel. You don't have to agree with it. What's important is will you stop hurting me?"

This is a clear question. It might be a scary one to pose, because what if he says no? But if that is indeed how he feels you might as well know it now and spare yourself additional inevitable hurt.

Assuming he says he will try to stop (which is the best you can expect—no one knows for sure how much or in what way they can change), move on to step number two.

DECIDE WHAT ACTIONS EACH OF YOU WILL TAKE TO CORRECT THINGS. Once you have explained how you feel about things and have established that you would both like the relationship to improve, you need to discuss how. You can't just leave it to chance.

In a way you have to make a "deal" so that each of you knows what to expect.

"I'm sorry you think I never listen when you talk to me." David sighed. "I do. I mean sometimes my mind wanders but lots of times it doesn't. What do you want me to do?"

Mary considered that for a long moment. "I guess I want you to try and concentrate a little more. I know you have stuff on your mind, but so do I. Maybe if you looked at me more when I'm talking . . . or weren't so silent. I can't tell that you're listening!"

"I'll try." David laughed. "I'll say, 'I'm still here!' every once in a while."

Mary didn't really think that was funny, but she laughed anyway, because it was apparent to her that David was trying.

"Well, maybe I could say, 'David, are you concentrating?' every once in a while. I promise I won't say it angrily if you don't get angry when I say it."

"Deal," David smiled, putting his arm around her.

Try and come up with different ways to resolve a problem that involve actions on both of your parts. It does take two to create a problem. (Watch your own behavior to see if you pay enough attention to him!) If he flirts too much and it drives you crazy, devise a signal you can send him to indicate he's doing it again and you don't like it. That will be his cue to stop.

If you tend to argue over his sports obligations on Saturday afternoons, try and find a compromise that respects his interests and your needs. You will agree not to complain he hasn't spent the day with you, and he will agree he won't go slumming after the game with his pals. Perhaps instead of getting annoyed when he goes off for his afternoon ball game in the park, you could come to watch the last quarter and bring along a snack picnic to enjoy together afterward.

You need to design a plan that puts you both in the "driver's seat." That empowers both of you. Otherwise each of you will simply be suspiciously lying in wait to see if the other is going to do as promised, instead of concentrating on each of your own responsibilities.

FOLLOW THROUGH ON YOUR ACTIONS AND SEE IF THINGS IMPROVE. Do what you have said you will do, and with your whole being. Don't just get your body to move to point A or B. Put your mind into it as well. Also, keep these ground rules in mind. . . .

- Expect things to be a bit awkward at first as you both try on new behaviors.
- Keep your sense of humor. If he lapses into

41

his absentminded ways or you find yourself becoming unfairly demanding, laugh
about it. A misstep is not the problem. Not
realizing you're doing it is.

- Don't expect things to change overnight.
  You may both need to get the hang of your
  new behaviors. You may both need to see
  the positive rewards of changing old behaviors to new ones.

- Don't keep trying endlessly with no results
  just because you want to hang onto a relationship. Things should improve pretty
  quickly. If the new behaviors come from
  the heart and are true to how the two of
  you feel about each other, then your relationship will blossom. But if only one (or
  neither) of you feel inspired from deep inside to change, than chances are the relationship will continue to falter. When
  things hardly improve, or do at first and
  then quickly deteriorate, you'll begin to
  sense this isn't working. You might want
  to hide from the fact, but don't. You will
  just be putting off the inevitable ... and
  possibly setting yourself up for even more
  hurt along the way.

ARE THERE ANY CLEAR SIGNS
THAT TWO PEOPLE SHOULD BREAK UP?

There are a number of classic signs that two
people should break up. But the signs are rarely
perfectly clear. The emotional attachment between the couple can be so strong that it's hard
to read any signs at all. Two people don't have

to be right or good for each other for them to find it hard to part. This is so for a number of reasons. People who should break up often don't because:

- Out of insecurity they might feel they won't find anyone else.
- They may simply be afraid of being alone.
- They may be somewhat addicted to the highly emotional storms that accompany the relationship (see chapters seven and eight.)
- Ending a relationship brings with it a special pain unrelated to that particular relationship itself. (Perhaps someone's parent, sibling, or other loved one has died and the break-up is bringing those awful feelings back.)
- If you've been physically close with someone it can strengthen an attachment.

Still, it's important to stay aware of what's going on in the relationship. Below are some signals that things are on a downward spiral:

- You keep getting into the same kinds of misunderstandings even though you've discussed the way in which you misread each other.
- Neither one of you seems able to really talk about the way you feel about anything— ever.
- When you are out with him you find yourself always longing to be with a good friend.

- You are consistently feeling hurt by his behavior.
- He is highly and unrelentingly critical of you.
- You feel tense every time you are about to get together.

The bottom line? Anytime you find yourself feeling consistently unhappy or dissatisfied or alone or hurt in the relationship it is likely time to break up. Understand though, the operative word here is "consistently." *This can't be stressed enough.* Every relationship has tough spots. It's when the problems don't go away, but rather continue or intensify despite your desire and efforts to make it otherwise that a break-up may be indicated.

Breaking up is never easy, but when you are hampered by all sorts of fears and insecurities and needs, it can make the decision even harder. There are many situations too that are neither black nor white which further complicate the situation. If you'd rather not break up there are many reasonable excuses for putting the possibly inevitable off. Sometimes things do work out!

Perhaps he's rather selfish. That can be difficult, but you might still be able to, in time, teach him to behave otherwise.

Maybe you don't feel relaxed together or as if you can talk about many things. Then again, maybe it will just take time for each of you to really open up.

Then too you may seem to be constantly at odds with each other. You may bicker a lot. But that could be the way you like to show affection.

Laughing, arguing, making up, and laughing again could be a pattern that keeps you excited and interested.

But there is one thing that is unacceptable and that no excuse will accommodate.

PHYSICAL OR EMOTIONAL ABUSE

There is no excuse for emotional or physical abuse good enough to warrant staying in a relationship.

What exactly is emotional or physical abuse? Is an occasional put down, or a hand squeezing your arm a little too hard during a terrible argument abuse?

Yes. And don't pretend it isn't. Certainly this kind of thing can happen between two people who otherwise treat each other well. If you believe it won't happen again you needn't necessarily do anything drastic. But don't pretend it hasn't been an abusive moment.

The trouble with some kinds of abuse is that since we don't want to believe it's happening to us, we label it something else. You might say, "He got a little rough." But when it happens again, you may do the same. You may have trouble ever calling it what it is. *Abuse.*

Constant put downs and insults meant to completely belittle you are abuse. Any sort of physical contact, such as a shove or an arm squeeze, or an outright physical action such as slapping, kicking, hitting, or pushing is abuse. Any time you walk away from your boyfriend feeling emotionally demeaned, physically hurt, or as if your safety has been compromised, you are being abused and you should not be with him.

This probably sounds very unsympathetic, and if it's someone you care very much about it will be hard to part. Especially if you know there are clear reasons why he behaves so cruelly . . . reasons you know are behind his need to put you down or to strike you physically.

A WORD ABOUT "DATE RAPE"

You've probably heard this expression before. It means something very specific and comes neatly under the heading of abuse.

When most people hear the word "rape," they think of a situation where a stranger forces sex upon his terrified victim. This is an accurate picture. But it's not the whole story. Rape, or "date rape" can also occur between two people who know each other. The rapist is not a stranger, and the victim is willingly on a date with him. For part of the evening things can feel innocent enough. So when he forces sex upon her, when he refuses to hear her "NO!" his victim (his date!) becomes frightened, deeply upset, and extremely confused. Is this her fault, she might think? Did I ask for this, she might wonder? Should I have let him kiss me?

The answer to these questions is simply this. If you're out on your first or fifth date with a boy and if when he suggests serious physical intimacy you say no and he doesn't listen but instead forces you with his strength to give him what he wants, this is date rape.

This is abuse.

It doesn't matter if you let him kiss you. That was a yes. It doesn't matter if you let him hug you. That was a yes, too. But when you say no, whenever that time comes, and he doesn't listen, you are being abused, and he is committing a crime.

But that doesn't mean he should be allowed to do so.

Even if someone is hurting him at home.

Even if you know he's depressed

Even if he swears he loves you.

Even if he says he couldn't be happy without you.

Even if he promises he'll never do it again.

And even if he claims you deserve it.

Because you don't. No one does.

If you don't want to leave a person who is physically and/or emotionally hurting you, you need to think about two things.

1) Why do you feel so attached to someone who hurts you? Does it feel familiar? Do you somehow think that this is the best you can expect, that you are really annoying, or ugly, or stupid? If your answer to any of these questions is yes it might be helpful for you to speak to a counselor at school, a favorite teacher, or a minister or rabbi. If possible, ask your parents about finding you a professional person who can help you gain a more positive sense of yourself.

2) The solution does not have to be completely walking away. You can advise your boyfriend to get some help himself. You can stay in touch. And you can tell him (and yourself) that if he is able to get himself under control, you would be willing to try seeing him again. But you do have to make it clear you will no longer tolerate mistreatment. That promises of it stopping don't mean anything to you. And that you think he needs help.

No one likes to make difficult decisions. But when the going gets rough in a relationship that's exactly what people feel like they have to do. Make a decision.

Other than an abusive situation however, the decision doesn't have to be one of staying together or not. It can first be a decision about what to do to improve things.

You might end up breaking up or you might not, but taking that interim step to work on your relationship will help you roll with whatever happens. (If you do break up after you both tried to make it work, parting will likely not be so difficult.)

Besides, even the best relationships, and even the big one leading to marriage, will have rocky times. You might as well polish your problem-solving skills so that every relationship to come can be as strong as possible.

Wonderful relationships are usually the result of two people joyfully sharing the good times and bravely allowing the bad to strengthen and deepen their feelings for each other.

FIVE

BREAKING UP KINDLY

There is no one good way to break up.

It all depends on you and your partner (your temperaments, your abilities to talk openly), the reasons you are splitting up (he cheated, you are both feeling trapped, your feelings are fading), how you feel about each other (break-ups can happen between people who still care a lot!), where you are (on the phone long distance, taking a walk, at the local pizza shop), and the way in which you'd like to break up (completely, still date each other, take a two-week break and then check back with each other to see what the feelings are).

Every situation is different.

However, the need for kindness, consideration, and generosity during a break-up remains constant. And it's an especially good idea if the two of you are hoping for a reconciliation.

Emotions usually run very high during a break-up and it is very easy to succumb to angry words, quick exits, insulting remarks, copious tears, and more. But you can minimize the chances of things reaching an unbearable temperature.

While there is no one perfect way to break up, there are still choices you can make and manners you can employ that will help both of you smooth the very rough edges of this difficult time.

Note: All suggested words and phrases are just that. Suggestions. They are intended to guide you toward a gentle, direct approach critical to a kind break-up. Still, every relationship is highly personal. You will want to make the words your own.

IF POSSIBLE, PICK A QUIET PLACE

Whether or not the break-up is expected, both of you will be more comfortable in a private space. One of you might cry. You might exchange angry words. You might even need to walk away from each other for a few moments to collect yourselves.

These are not things you will want to do in a public place. Obvious displays of emotion will capture too much attention. People will stare curiously. If someone you know sees you they will likely repeat what they've seen and heard to others. Pretty soon your private time together will become common knowledge . . . before either of you have had a chance to cope with what's happened.

Also, public spaces can be inhibiting. Aware that others are around you might not say exactly what you'd like. Or you may behave in a way that fails to reflect how you truly feel.

So don't break up at a dance, or at a local hangout or in front of a group of friends. You will end up hurting each other and entertaining everyone else. This is a time for the two of you to say what you need to say and to express your emotions in a way that respects the gravity of the moment. Take a quiet walk, or find a private place in the park, or meet at a coffee shop most kids don't frequent. That way you can concentrate on each other and not worry about anything or anyone else.

HONESTY IS GOOD, BUT FULL DISCLOSURE OFTEN ISN'T

You will want to be as straightforward and honest about how you are feeling as possible. But there is a line over which it is not good or kind or helpful to cross. When you move from speaking the basic truth, to offering painful details, you may be unnecessarily hurting your soon-to-be-ex. And you may inadvertently set the stage for an ugly scene, or a situation in which it would be impossible to reconcile (even if you think you won't want to, you never know!). It's important to speak the truth, but do so in a measured fashion.

- If you're thinking, I've outgrown him, say something like, "I feel as if we've been moving in different directions. I have this sense that I'm changing and I'm not sure where I fit right now . . ." You will have avoided insulting him and instead placed the "blame" on your own—changing—self.

- If you're thinking, I've met someone else I

like more, say something like, "I think I'm not really ready to just hang out with one person. I think you're great, but it's me. I'm not comfortable right now with the idea of going exclusively with someone." There's no point making him feel perfectly dreadful that someone else has entered the picture. He'll see you dating soon enough. Hearing that you don't want to be tied down is far easier to take. And maybe it's really the truth. You may not like being tied down to the new guy either!

- If you're thinking, I just don't like you anymore, say something like, "I've started to feel like we don't have that much in common. I don't feel as connected as I used to and I'm not sure why. I just have this sense that I need to be on my own now for a while." Telling a person you don't like them anymore can be extremely hurtful. Putting the break-up in terms of your own confusion over what you're feeling is a much gentler way to go.

- If you're thinking, I'd like to still date, but I want to see other guys too, try saying, "Look. I still like you a lot. But I'm just feeling as if I need to be free to spend more time with my friends, and even maybe see another guy sometimes. I want to experience different things. But I still really like spending time with you and I'm wondering if we could still go out every once in a while?" By making it perfectly clear that you still enjoy his company, you will stack the odds in your favor that he will agree.

(Maybe not on the spot. He has his pride. But sometime later . . .)

AVOID ANYTHING IMPULSIVE

Even if you've caught your boyfriend kissing another girl. Even if he embarrasses you for the third time in front of some friends. Even if he always seems to put his own needs before yours and this last decision, the last minute decision to go the football game instead of to a concert with you, is the last straw . . . don't break up on the spot.

It would be most unkind . . . to you.

Ending a meaningful relationship is a painful thing to do, and is made easier only by your ability to understand what's happened and to express yourself fully and completely. Walking off in a rage and refusing to speak gives neither one of you a chance to say things that might need to be said, and which might lead to an easier break, or even a relationship filled with more understanding.

● ―――――――――――――――――――――――――――― ●

Jessica could not believe her eyes. Greg, her boyfriend of three months, was sitting in a back booth of Giorgio's Pizza with a girl. His arm was draped loosely around her shoulders.

Jessica snapped.

Angrily she began walking towards them, completely unsure of what she would say when she got there. Her mind was buzzing and her heart was beating in her ears. Greg did not see her approach.

"Hello," she said flatly, now standing next to the table.

"J . . . Jessica," Greg said, clearly startled.

"Nice," Jessica said sarcastically.

"I . . . I . . ." Greg stammered and then looked down at the table.

"Don't ever speak to me again," Jessica spat out, and then turned on her heels and walked away. He tried calling her three times after that but she would never take his phone calls. She was too humiliated. Too worried about what others were saying. Shutting Greg out seemed the only way to keep her pride. She cried every night though for six weeks.

A few months after that Jessica was talking to Greg's friend and he revealed something she hadn't known. Greg had been miserable without her, but furious she wouldn't give him a chance to explain. The girl had been a camp girlfriend from a neighboring town. He'd gone out with her for old times' sake and had never intended for Jessica to know. It wasn't a big romantic thing, and Greg had missed Jessica terribly. But he had also been furious she wouldn't let him explain . . . or apologize.

◆━━━━━━━━━━━━━━━━━━━━━◆

It's important to talk out differences. Lots of times you can get so caught up with your own problems, dreams, and anxieties that it's easy to forget there's another side. That other people have problems too and that they may not always behave the way we'd like. It doesn't mean they're bad, or don't care about us. Impulsive reactions can rob you of ever really knowing what happened, or of the comfort of understanding the whole emotional picture.

WHEN SOMEONE IS BREAKING UP WITH YOU

The goal here is to be kind to yourself. Even if someone is breaking up with you, it's important to recognize that you can still maintain some control. Your behavior during and directly after the break-up can go a long way toward caring for yourself—no matter what he says or does:

- Don't ask whether or not he's met someone else and what she has that you don't. First of all, the fact that he was open to meeting someone else is the real problem. If it wasn't this girl it would have been another. Even if there is another girl, he will probably not admit it, and if he does admit it, you'll feel dreadful. Also asking what she has that you don't will likely not elicit an answer (unless your ex is a real creep.) Which is good because whatever he might say won't really be the whole picture. Anyway, if he needed to move on, and experience another girlfriend, the main thing to remember is that what this girl has going for her is that she's not you!

- Don't, especially if this break-up is a big surprise, become hysterical. Big, powerful reactions are scary. They might make him so nervous that he says any number of things he doesn't entirely mean. "This really has to be over," he might blurt out. "I just don't care as much as you do . . ." he might say.

- Don't bargain. Don't suggest that you just see each other every once in a while. In the end, if he really intends to break up, you will only be prolonging the torture. Besides, if it's not an arrangement you really like, you shouldn't accept it. Just because he's decided he wants to break up, doesn't mean you are any less of a person than the one he started dating. Don't suggest you're willing to keep dating until he's made up his mind about you or this other girl. Don't tell him what you think your faults are and how you are willing to change if he'll just give it one more shot. If he's breaking up with you it's because he wants to. Even if he's sorry tomorrow, this is what he wants right now. Trying to bargain (or argue) will only make you feel small and "less than."

- Don't ask him what he doesn't like about you anymore. It doesn't matter. You can't and shouldn't ache to change for him. What he doesn't like, someone else will one day love. Besides, why would you want to sit and listen to a litany of what he considers to be your problems? After all, he's got some too.

- Don't be on the attack. Communicate your willingness to try and make this as easy for the two of you as possible. If you respond with, "I can't believe you're doing this!" or "You are a horrible person!" you will probably hear some very hurtful remarks that will only serve to make you feel worse.

There are however, many things you should do which will help you cope with the immediate event and even go a long way toward easing the aftermath. You will need a measure of calm and understanding as you try to cope with the actual break-up, and making use of the following suggestions will help:

DO: Take your time. Think through what you want to say. Comments that first spring to mind are not necessarily the ones that should spring from your lips.

DO: If he says he needs more room, or needs to date other girls, ask him in what ways the relationship has been making him feel boxed in. The information will help you see how the expectations that you had might or might not have been more flexible.

DO: If he has been treating you in an unpleasant way, tell him so. You will want to express your anger or resentment so the feelings don't fester inside you, creating even more anger or worse, a stubborn depression. Try to express yourself calmly and without much drama. It will force him to talk in a straightforward manner. You may learn quite a bit more about what makes him tick . . . and why you might be better off without him.

DO: Tell him that you're hurt. (If you're surprised he's breaking it off, say that, too.) And if you think he hasn't tried awfully hard to make things work, let him know it. The point is to say what's on your mind so that you don't feel too bottled up. You're going to feel that way a little anyway. The immediate pain of a break-up is intense and it's not a good idea to let all of it out. But if there are specific things that you resent, saying them, even if you'd rather *Shout* them, will help to relieve the internal pressure.

COMPLICATED BREAK-UP SITUATIONS

Some break-up situations are particularly sticky. Your boyfriend may have gotten involved with your friend. You may have fallen for your boyfriend's buddy. You may be moving away and can't find the right words to explain that you will want to feel free to date others. He may be crazy about you and another girl at the same time and find himself totally confused about what to do.

Complicated situations require some extra thought. Clear thinking will only help minimize the drama and maximize a constructive outcome.

IF YOUR BOYFRIEND HAS GOTTEN INVOLVED WITH YOUR GIRLFRIEND

You're going to feel angry and doubly betrayed. It may seem as if you will never trust anyone again. But there is another way to look at it.

Your boyfriend drifted off because he wasn't really ready to be committed to you. Your girlfriend fell for him, not to be mean to you, but because she couldn't ignore her attraction for him. It hurts, and you will undoubtedly feel they handled the situation poorly. And probably they did. It's not an easy thing to handle well. But it doesn't mean they are terrifically dishonest people or that everyone else is too.

Tell your boyfriend you think he should have been straight with you about not wanting to be a "couple" before he hurt you by going off with someone else. And tell your girlfriend, you would have expected her to stand away from him until he had ended things with you. Do this as evenly as you can. And then embrace your pride and put some distance between you and them. "You're a backstabber!" or "You purposefully lied to me!" will only, when the inevitable argument is over, make you feel as if you revealed too much of your inner self. Keep your head high and give yourself credit for not stooping to angry accusations.

YOU'VE FALLEN FOR YOUR BOYFRIEND'S BUDDY

If you've fallen for your boyfriend's buddy, whether you've acted yet or not, it means your relationship with your boyfriend is no longer one you should be in. Don't wait to see if the relationship between you and this new guy can work. Gently break up with your boyfriend as soon as possible. It isn't fair to use him as a safety net if things don't work out with the friend. However, if you've already gotten involved with the buddy, you can't exactly ignore that and simply break up with your old boyfriend (even if your words are kind).

You will have to tell him the truth. But do so being as sensitive as possible about your change in affections for him. "When things started not to feel right between us I guess I began to think

59

about other guys. And the truth is I found myself feeling interested in Peter. I'm telling you this because I don't want you to just see us doing stuff together and feel as if I lied to you. It would have been better if we'd separated when I began to feel uncomfortable and before Peter, but I guess I was chicken and I knew I still liked you and I guess I hoped it would get better. That wasn't very straightforward of me. I'm sorry."

YOU'RE MOVING AWAY AND YOUR BOYFRIEND WANTS YOU TO STAY LOYAL

If you and your boyfriend are at odds about what should happen when you are physically separated (and this includes summer vacations) rather than leave each other angrily, try agreeing to see how you feel once you are parted. It can be frightening to feel so close to someone and then suddenly be separated. Part of your boyfriend's desire for you to stay loyal is his fear of being alone, missing you, and then being speedily replaced. But once he has time to get back on his feet he may settle into a more realistic expectation. Do promise to communicate honestly when you are away from each other so that neither one of you believes something of the relationship that isn't true.

YOU LIKE YOUR BOYFRIEND TREMENDOUSLY. HE LIKES YOU TOO, BUT THERE'S ANOTHER GIRL HE LIKES JUST AS MUCH. HE CAN'T DECIDE WHAT TO DO AND NEITHER CAN YOU.

Part of you will probably want to stay, be super wonderful to him, and hope he chooses you. Another part of you would probably like to say,

"Oh yeah? Well, who needs this?" and then just walk away for good.

The problem is both possibilities are destructive. The first will leave you feeling worthless while you are attempting to be the most glittering prize. Trying to win someone's love can whittle away at your self-worth. No relationship can be truly happy when one person feels "less than." On the other hand, running away angrily will always leave you wondering what might have happened if you'd given him a little room and yourself a touch more dignity. (This is a situation that can potentially be very hurtful to your pride. But only if you let it. Refusing to try and "win" someone and resisting the temptation to run can leave you feeling strong and proud.)

So what other possibilities are there? First, remind yourself he's not so sure he wants to lose you either. Then, consider these moves:

♣ If you can handle his indecision (which truthfully doesn't make him a bad person), you might want to say, "Okay. Look. I can't say I'm going to wait for you. If you want to see her I'll be going out too and then we'll see how we both feel . . ."

♣ If you feel too hurt to continue seeing him while he sees someone else you might say, "Look, I can't go from being each other's only person, to suddenly having a third person around. I'm hurt that you want to date someone else. But you go ahead and do it. Stopping you wouldn't work. You'll see how you feel and where I am when you figure out what you want."

● If you just don't know what you can handle or what you can't, try suggesting that
you continue seeing each other but with
some real advance planning so that there's
no question on your part as to whether
he's seeing you or her a particular afternoon or evening. Point out that you too
can make other social plans for yourself
and will keep him informed. Agree that
you will see how it goes with the understanding that you may have to completely
back away from each other and leave it to
"the fates."

Break-ups can happen in many different ways.
The most important thing to keep in mind is
kindness and thoughtfulness.
It protects everyone's ego.
It preserves dignity.
It expresses caring and concern.
And no matter which side of the break-up you
are on, it will leave you feeling like a responsible
and quality person. If you are doing the breaking
up you won't walk away feeling like a creep, and
if you're being left, you won't walk away feeling
belittled by your venomous reaction.
Moving forward will be that much easier. . . .

SIX

GETTING DUMPED AND SURVIVING IT

The aftermath of a break-up, especially one which you do not initiate, can be devastating. There are a myriad of emotions you might experience:

Loneliness: You've been used to having someone special in your life, and now, suddenly, he's not there. The phone doesn't ring quite as much. Saturday afternoons or evenings are once again a question mark.

Hurt: It's very painful to yearn for someone who for any number of reasons has walked away. The feelings of desertion and rejection can be quite powerful.

Anxiety: All kinds of questions can hound you after a break-up. Will I ever meet anyone I like again? What will everyone think of me? Did I do something terribly wrong? Am I, somehow, not good enough?

This last question is probably the most painful and unfortunately common reaction to an unwanted break-up. "What does this break-up say about me?" is the kind of torturous thought most everyone entertains when they feel "dumped."

In fact it is a reflection of the single worst thing that can happen after a break-up. Self-doubt.

Getting over a break-up is a step-by-step process. And it begins with putting those "I-guess-I'm-not-so-lovable" feelings to rest.

STEP ONE: KEEP YOUR SELF-DOUBT UNDER CONTROL

The first thing you will have to set straight in your mind after "getting dumped" is what it *doesn't* say about you. As stated earlier, it's all too easy to conclude that if you'd only been prettier, or smarter, or more independent, or funnier, or more interesting, or less demanding, or more intellectual the break-up wouldn't have happened. But this simply isn't true. And if you find yourself convinced that it is, consider the following.

WHAT BREAK-UPS DON'T MEAN

<u>IF YOU'D BEEN PRETTIER, SMARTER, FUNNIER, EVERYTHING WOULD HAVE BEEN FINE.</u> Clearly your boyfriend thinks you're attractive. Otherwise he wouldn't have been interested in the first place. And yes, when you first started going out, at a time when people are most "star struck," he might have thought you more beautiful than he does now. But you can bet that's not the reason he broke up with you. The same goes for your intelligence and sense of humor. The "package" that is you did not just disappear. You are you. What your boyfriend needed changed.

IF YOU'D BEEN A BETTER GIRLFRIEND—MORE INDEPEN-
DENT, INTERESTING, SURE OF YOURSELF—EVERYTHING
WOULD HAVE BEEN FINE. You might have been the
most perfect girlfriend in the world and the
break-up still would have happened. You also
might have been the worst and ended up dump-
ing *him*! Whether or not you and your boyfriend
could stay together could not possibly be completely dependent on you alone. It takes two people to make a relationship work and fall apart.
It's a partnership, not a solo act. Even if you were
too dependent, perhaps in subtle ways he en-
couraged it and then realized he didn't like it.
Maybe you weren't sure enough of yourself, because he was never quite able to be there the way
you needed him to be. You don't behave the way
you do in a vacuum. He's right there along with
you.

ONCE ANY GUY GETS TO KNOW THE REAL YOU, HE'LL AL-
WAYS DUMP YOU. Once you really get to know anyone else, you'll find out all manner of things
about them, both good and bad. Loving anyone,
wanting to be with them always, entails accept-
ing flaws. It also takes a certain maturity. The
real you is full of wonderful surprises. But you
wouldn't be human if the real you didn't exist
with a number of characteristics that disappoint
you and others. The problem is that when people
are young they think they are going to find Mr.
and Ms. Perfect. So when things go wrong or
they feel disappointed, they often think, "Uh oh,
I'd better look elsewhere." This doesn't mean the
real you is a problem. It means the real you isn't
perfect. Neither is your *real* boyfriend. But he'll
find all this out soon enough.

Self-doubt can be endless torture.

It can make the painful aftermath of a break-up go on and on and on.

The first step toward moving past the pain is to stop inflicting it on yourself.

STEP TWO: REACH OUT TO YOUR GIRLFRIENDS

When boys first enter your life it may feel as if nothing could be more exciting ... or important. Girl friendships may at times seem to fade in comparison.

But hopefully you will see early on that boyfriends and girlfriends each have an important place in your life. And that each kind of relationship needs nurturing.

What does "nurturing" mean? In this case, paying attention. When you have a boyfriend, hopefully you've also been checking in with your girlfriends, seeing if you can help with their problems, and spending special time together.

This will naturally make it easier for you to turn to your girlfriends during difficult times. They won't feel used. They will know you cared during the good times, so they won't mind helping you during the bad.

You needn't spill every feeling to all of them. Some people can be expected to keep a confidence better than others. But don't be afraid to admit to feeling insecure, or dumped, or rejected. Everyone will have these feelings during the course of their love life. And by sharing your emotions honestly you will make your relationship with your girlfriends deeper and more meaningful.

Which is exactly what you need right now.

But what if you've been less than attentive while dating? You may have trouble unburdening yourself to a girlfriend. Now that you need her, she may not be so willing to just get close again. After all, when you get your next boyfriend, maybe you'll disappear once more.

The thing is, however, you need your girlfriends now, so there's only one thing you can do.

Face your mistake and try to mend things.

Call a friend whom you think is particularly understanding and forgiving, and say, "I know I haven't been paying a lot of attention to you and I know that wasn't right. I'm sorry. I won't let this happen again. But do you think we can talk? David and I have broken up and I feel so horrible."

Chances are she'll be happy to see you.

She might not be if you just launched into your problems without ever acknowledging how you might have made her feel by your inattentiveness. She needs to know you recognize your own hurtful behavior toward her and that you would likely not make that mistake again.

STEP THREE: HAVE A GOOD CRY, OR SCREAMFEST

Let it out. If you have intense feelings give them some physical and emotional expression. Don't be afraid to be dramatic. You can do this yourself or in front of a friend. You will need to release your feelings before you can really start coping with them constructively.

So cry into a pillow, or throw them around the room, or if this is more your style, sit in a dark room and feel horribly, desperately miserable and sorry for yourself.

Whatever your mode, give it full flower.

Don't be afraid if you start you'll never stop. Actually the opposite is true. If you don't get it out the pain won't stop.

STEP FOUR: WRITE A LETTER

Especially if you've managed to control your anger and hurt and not say or do anything vicious and unfair, chances are you're sitting on a lot of unspoken words. There might be many things you would have liked to have said, which would have hurt your ex, or expressed just how furious you are, or exaggerated your indignation but would have felt great anyway.

You don't want these unspoken words to eat you up alive.

So put them down on paper.

Be as vicious or vindicative or hurtful as you'd like. Say it all. Even the stuff you don't really mean. Then put it in an envelope and put it in your drawer.

Periodically over the next few days pull it out and read it. Revise it if you like. Add things here, take away things there.

Say it out loud. Read it silently.

Do this as often as you'd like.

Amazingly, you will begin to relax. You will have thought the thoughts, said the words, added the drama of your outraged voice and done so over and over and over. Even though your ex will not have seen a thing or heard a word, a sense of satisfaction will begin to descend upon you.

Also a sense of control. You got out your deepest feelings without compromising your integrity.

STEP FIVE: ACCEPT THE FACT THAT YOU'RE GOING TO HURT

If you try and run from the hurt, the pain will only come out in other ways, causing unexpected problems. The fact is, if you are hurt you have no reasonable choice but to face it. Too many other areas of your life will be affected if you don't.

●━━━━━━━━━━━━━━━━━━━●

Nina walked away from Peter stunned. She'd known things weren't perfect between them, but still she had no idea he had been that unhappy. He hadn't even wanted to talk about it! He just wanted out.

As soon as Nina got home she called her good friend Victoria.

"Wow, you must feel awful!" Victoria cried out.

Nina was about to say yes when something stopped her.

"Why," she told herself, "should I feel bad? Peter is the loser! He threw away something great."

"Not in the least," Nina declared proudly.

"What a jerk. Let's do something next weekend. You know. Look for new guys at Victor's Pizza."

"Great idea," Victoria replied. "I can't believe you! You're so together!"

"I am," Nina practically sang out. "See you tomorrow!"

"What do you mean?" Victoria asked.

"Tomorrow's Saturday. We're going shopping, remember?" Nina responded quickly. A little tensely too.

"Oh, Nina, I'm sorry!" Victoria sighed. "I told Mr. Jakes I'd babysit. I really need the money. I forgot!"

"Oh, that's just great," Nina snapped. "Thanks . . ."

Victoria hesitated. "Nina. You know I need to make some pocket money . . . Please don't be like that."

"I just think you should keep the plans you make," Nina charged forward, vaguely aware she wasn't being nice. Or sympathetic. Or generous.

But somehow she just couldn't stop. . . .

●━━━━━━━━━━━━━━━━━━━━━━━━━●

Lots of people prefer to run from pain. Hurt is hard to handle and so they try to pretend they simply don't feel it.

Bad idea.

Hurt is part of life. And the only way to get over it is to experience it. Certainly there are a lot of ways to *try* and run from the pain, but the end result is usually a problem.

You might quickly get another boyfriend but then discover you don't really care about him or he, you, and you end up with another different kind of unpleasant break-up.

You might force yourself into a good mood but end up snapping at good friends for no good reason.

You may become absentminded and somewhat ineffective in your pursuits. (You might botch a test, lose a race, miss a basket, fail to remember a good friend's invitation, and more.)

You will likely feel generally off balance and "revved up," using a lot of your psychic energy to hide from the hurt rather than work it through.

Running from unhappy truths doesn't change the facts. But it can complicate your life a lot. Better to deal with what you are dealt and then simply move on.

STEP SIX: PUT ON A NOT-HAPPY, NOT-SAD FACE

It's not that it matters what people think. It's a question of you feeling better or worse as a consequence of what you project. Quite simply, if you behave as if you are devastated, it will keep you feeling that way. Wearing your heart on your sleeve might feel honest, but it might also ultimately leave you feeling embarrassed by everyone's awareness of your pain. If you let your stronger side step forward, a few friends and you will be aware of your vulnerability, but you will also be reminded of your more solid self. It's important to let down your guard with some people. Letting out your true feelings can be a wonderful release. But projecting the idea that you can handle the break-up, that you're not ashamed of it, that you still think you're good, will not only convince others of these facts, but more importantly, you!

STEP SEVEN: RECOGNIZE THAT YOU NEED TIME TO RECOVER

It will be tempting to leap into another relationship as quickly as possible, but don't do it!

You need time to get over the hurt, to see that being on your own is not such a terrible thing, and to gain back your self-confidence through light dating. You should spend time with friends and enjoy interesting or fun activities. There's a good reason for this approach.

● If you jump into another relationship very quickly, you might be doing so to prove you're still pretty or fun or smart. Then, because the relationship won't have begun out of mutual deep caring, you will likely run into compatibility problems. Soon you'll be breaking up again, and your self-confidence will plummet even further.

● Going out with other guys with no intention of a serious relationship developing will give you a chance to feel some excitement in your life without placing your ego on the line. You need that. A good, fun time without worrying "what he thinks" will give you a chance to just think about yourself. Not what he expects or wants. Not what you wish you were. But just about yourself and what you need to do to have a good time.

- Exploring new or old favorite activities, hanging out with friends or making new ones will afford you an opportunity to see that you *can* stand on your own without feeling totally lonely or bored or unimportant.

Surviving a break-up should not just be about getting over feelings of rejection. It should also be about strengthening friendships, becoming better acquainted with your own strengths, and learning new and important things about love and romance.

So don't just think of it as a depressing, horrible process that needs to take place before the next boyfriend comes along. Rather, consider it a time of strong feelings, exploration, and change.

Then you won't just be surviving. You'll be triumphing!

BUT WHAT IF YOU'RE THE ONE DOING THE BREAKING UP?

Most people assume that if they're the ones doing the breaking up, they are not entitled to difficult feelings.

But that's not true.

If you've just ended a relationship you might have all kinds of unhappy thoughts.

You are entitled. It's a dissapointing loss even if it's one you are convinced has to happen.

You might feel guilty that you hurt your ex.

You may feel uncertain about your decision.

You may actually regret the break-up because being on your own feels so strange now.

You might feel angry or hurt. You might have done the breaking up because your ex betrayed or hurt you in some way. In other words, you might feel dumped even though you said good-bye first.

Whether or not your friends recognize your right to sympathy or support, you should know you deserve to be kind to yourself. You too need time to find your balance, to miss and mourn what was, and to take what's happened and learn from it.

Being close with someone is a wonderful feeling. Parting isn't. It doesn't matter what side of the fence you are on, saying good-bye carries some degree of sorrow with it.

The trick is to keep your feelings limited to the sadness and upset over what has happened, and away from self-doubt and criticism.

No one deserves that.

SEVEN

THE RELATIONSHIP THAT JUST WON'T GO AWAY

Sometimes you may mean to break up. You may realize things aren't going well. Your boyfriend doesn't really understand you or you, him. He's expressed his dissatisfaction. You've agreed it's probably time to part, and to see other people and just be friends.

But somehow that's not what's happening.

Instead you seem to be repeatedly getting back together. Maybe it's just for an evening. Sometimes for as long as a few days. It's not that you're happiest together either.

It's that somehow you feel relieved to be connected once more.

Part of a pair.

So what's going on? Is this what love is about?

No, it isn't. This is what *dependence* is about.

WHAT'S BEHIND THE "WE'RE ON, WE'RE OFF" SYNDROME

First, as stated earlier, it's never easy to part from someone with whom you have been close. Even if there has been a growing distance be-

75

tween you, the memories of intimate conversations or secrets shared or physical closeness can still linger.

Playing these moments over in your mind, the two of you may begin to miss the sweetness and warmth of the romance. Pretty soon you might actually yearn for each other once more.

Or you may be having trouble meeting anyone else you like, or find yourself interested in someone who isn't interested in you.

Or you might just feel happiest when connected to a boy.

And so you go back to your ex, ignoring the bad times of the past and hoping for the best in the future.

Unfortunately, shortly thereafter you discover the same problems you had before cropping up again, and creating a rift between you. And so you part, and perhaps a few days later start to miss the good times once more.

This is not a good sign. In fact, you could be causing yourself a bit more trouble than you know.

●————————————————————————————●

Kara and Barry had broken up last month largely because they didn't seem able to talk. At first they had felt very excited about the relationship and could barely get enough of each other's company . . . and kisses. But then after about a month Kara began to realize Barry didn't seem all that interested when she tried to speak of her feelings of jealousy for her older sister. Or about her parents' divorce. It was as if Barry was, well, bored.

Kara told him about the impression she was getting, but he didn't seem to grasp it. "I like you a lot," he'd said, "but you get kind of depressing." The relationship dragged on for another month and then they decided to break up. But after a week, Kara started to feel very shaky. She was lonely on her own. And so she called Barry. He said he was beginning to miss her. And so they got back together. But then ten days later Kara once again found herself sitting across a table at the pizza shop from Barry, trying to figure out what to say or not say. She didn't want to . . . depress him. She didn't want to break up again. She needed his . . . his . . . Kara couldn't finish the thought. The truth was she needed nothing of Barry except his title. The boyfriend.

THE PROBLEM WITH NEVER SAYING GOOD-BYE

The central problem with breaking up and getting back together, only to break up again, is that this kind of pattern is usually indicative of two people who are afraid of being on their own.

As long as you remain afraid of being without a romance, of being a girl without a guy, you will likely continue falling back into old relationships and in so doing create all kinds of problems for yourself:

- You may cause yourself repeated pain as you and your ex struggle to make it work.
- You may miss chances to meet other guys.

- You may fail to give yourself a chance to see that being on your own can be fun.

- You may become so fearful of being on your own that you throw yourself into a relationship with someone new who might also be all wrong for you.

Obviously, you don't really want to chance any of the above.

So what can you do to keep from falling back into that old relationship?

Try and get control of those feelings of dependence.

HOW TO FEEL OKAY WITHOUT A BOY

You may always feel that you are happiest when you're romantically involved with someone. That's fine. In fact it's downright understandable. Why shouldn't you feel wonderful when there is a special person in your life with whom you can share love?

The trick is to still be able to feel happiness and experience a sense of security when there isn't a guy around. You don't need to be as "thrilled" as you might feel with a hot romance, but it's important to know you can enjoy yourself on your own.

You will want to break the "dependency" habit. Below are some tips for keeping your ex, your ex:

- Make a list of the things about him you didn't like. Read them over every time you have a desire to call.

- Make a list of all the feelings you had with him that hurt. Read them over every time you have a desire to make a date.

- Make a special effort to put yourself out there. Feelings of dependency can lead to feelings of embarrassment, which in turn can make you want to hide. You have nothing to feel embarrassed about. Everyone breaks up. Everyone spends time on their own. And then everyone eventually gets connected again. You both need to discover you can do fine on your own, and put yourself in a position to meet as many other guys as possible.

- Tell your friends how you are feeling. But do so in a way that makes you feel strong. "I'm so lonely," said with a sad voice and teary eyes may feel a little embarrassing. But, "I really need to be around my friends today!" won't. Both are the truth. But one has a much more positive "spin."

- Don't feel as if you have to shut your ex completely out. That might only build your desire to be with him. Rather, occasionally catch up with him in the hallways or park or pizza shop and say hello. You will likely be gently reminded of some of his traits you dislike, without having to actually date him again to reacquaint yourself with the problems.

So far we've discussed continuously returning to an old relationship because there is no one else, or because you want a boyfriend. It's not that you miss this particular guy all that much.

But what if you do? What if someone breaks up with you and now you just can't believe it's over. You miss him. You want him back. You can't believe how much.

This fixation can be very painful. You may have moved past being dependent on someone and ventured into the realm of obsession.

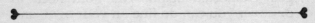

Consider the following questions. A yes answer to any might mean you have indeed become consumed by your ex.

1. Do you dream day and night about a guy who is no longer making himself available to you?

2. Do you believe that if you go after this boy in just the "right" way, he will once again be yours?

3. Did the rejection you experienced with him seem to make you feel even more passion for him than you did during the actual relationship?

4. Do you feel as if he's mistreating you because he won't give you what you want?

5. Do you find yourself calling him or com-

ing by his house with little excuses all the
time?

6. Do you regularly ask your friends if
they've seen him with anyone and how he
looks and what he says?

7. Do you believe this is the only guy you
can ever love?

If you answered any of these questions with
a yes, chances are you have crossed the line
from merely being a little dependent to being
obsessed.

This is not a good place to be.

•————————————————————•

Obsessions can be very destructive. They color
the way you see things. Nothing is clear. Everything is viewed through the idea that "I have to
have him." You may treat friends sloppily without knowing it. You may receive an insult from
the object of your obsession and not even hear
it. You may be unable to concentrate on other
things such as school, or family life, or even
yourself! It can affect your eating habits and your
mood and force all kinds of interests right out
the window.

If you think you're becoming obsessed with
someone, understand that trying to get over it
won't be easy. But it's much better than suffering
every day, wanting someone you can't have, and
who probably isn't who you think he is anyway.

And this is key.

The object of your obsession is very likely
quite different from the image you hold of him.
You have undoubtedly painted a picture in your

mind that addresses your every dream and desire.

But it is highly unlikely that this boy is equal to the image you have created.

So since this is true, why waste so much time wanting something that isn't real? Below is a five-step plan for shaking loose of your intense, never-ending desire to get back with the "perfect" guy.

STEP ONE: WHAT SETS YOU OFF?

Usually there are "triggers" for those moments when you find yourself consumed by thoughts of him—when you're sure there must be a way to get him back. Maybe it's when you open your drawer and see his picture. It could be the sweater you wore on your first date, or a romantic movie you saw together or even the table you used to sit at together in the pizza shop.

Keep track of what your triggers might be. Once you have a pretty good idea of what sparks endless thoughts of him, pack those items away or stay away from love stories, or sit on the opposite side of the local restaurant.

Tuck your triggers out of sight.

STEP TWO: PLAN A MENTAL MINIVACATION

You need to shift gears. You can absolutely tell yourself it's temporary. But decide to put him out of your head for about ten days. You will make no plans to win him back, and spend no time convincing yourself it can't *really* be over. Call it an experiment, or an exercise. Call it whatever you want. Keep in mind that you can always go back to thinking about him night and day. But now push all thoughts of him away. Any time you feel them creeping back, try and change the channel. Say to yourself "No. Not now." Then call a friend, or pick up a magazine or turn on the television.

ALTERNATIVE STEP TWO: IF YOU HAVE TO OBSESS, KEEP IT SHORT

It might be too hard to just make up your mind to put all thoughts of him aside. Your mind may tend to drift, and pushing visions of him away could require the strength of wild horses.

So don't push the thoughts away. There's no point spending all your energy constantly trying to fight them off. Doing so will only have the effect of keeping him on your mind. Rather, give your thoughts full reign. But only for a specific, concentrated amount of time. Twenty minutes, right after you get home from school, or ten minutes after dinner, or fifteen minutes as you're dressing in the morning. Try to plan it so that this special time is followed by an activity. It will help put closure on your thoughts.

STEP THREE: GET A FRIEND TO HELP

Enlist the help of a friend whom you can really trust. Tell her what you are trying to accomplish and ask if she can be the one to help you stay on track. Next time you feel like calling him, or are just thinking about him, call her instead. When you say something like, "I'm doing it again!" it will be her signal to remind you why you shouldn't—"He's not what you think he is. You would not be happy with him."—and then to help you think about something else entirely.

STEP FOUR: WHEN YOUR VACATION IS OVER
TRY ON NEW GLASSES

Now that you've given yourself that ten-day break, take another look. Think back. Chances are things might look a little different . . . if not simply because you got through an entire two weeks on your own, with very few thoughts of him to keep you going. Then do the following things:

Draw up a list of the difficult feelings you were spared these two weeks. (Jealousy, rejection, abandonment, etc.)

Draw up a list of all the problems that were in your relationship which you have, to date, ignored. (Never could be honest with each other, he was always hurting your feelings, etc.)

Draw up a list of all the true signs that this relationship has to be over. (You don't really miss the hurt, he's showing signs of interest in another girl, you envy your friend who has a loving relationship with a really nice guy, and you want that too, etc.)

STEP FIVE: WRITE A STORY TO YOURSELF ENTITLED:
THE HISTORY OF JIM AND ME, AND WHY
WE HAVE TO SAY GOOD-BYE

Describe in this memo, lovingly if you'd like, the beginning of your relationship. Then, as if you're writing a short story, track the details of your time together and when and how things started to go badly. Then describe in full detail how the break-up took place and all the feelings you experienced before, during, and after. Finally write down what you now perceive to be the truth about your relationship, pointing out what you'll miss and what you won't.

Then place this story in a safe place. It is your clearheaded record of the beginning, middle, and end of your relationship, and may be helpful to reread in a moment of loneliness when thinking about getting Jim back seems like a wonderful idea. . . .

ONE FINAL POINT ABOUT RELATIONSHIPS THAT WON'T GO AWAY

You may find yourself clinging to a relationship for reasons you don't fully understand. Perhaps there are problems at home and your deep feelings for a boy may have more to do with your urgent desire to feel safe. You may have lots of insecurities and need someone to prove to you that you're terrific. Something about a particular boy may remind you of someone in your family from whom you do not feel love or acceptance. Somehow capturing this boy feels as if it would take that pain away.

Whatever the reason, if you cannot let go of your dreams or fantasies about a particular boy, you might want to talk to your parents about finding a counselor or therapist who could help you get to the bottom of the problem.

It's important to get on with your life. Hanging on to the past is no way to move forward.

EIGHT

THE DATING-AGAIN TROUBLESHOOTER

Two months ago Barry suddenly broke up with you. It seemed to come out of nowhere. You hadn't expected it at all. This was very scary. How had you not known?

What does this say about you?

Or try this.

What if the break-up was expected and yet you still felt utterly blown away? Knocked off your feet? What does that mean?

Break-ups can reveal things about yourself you never knew. They can teach you things about life you never understood before. And they can make you awfully worried about coping with the next relationship and possible break-up.

Past break-ups can scare you off of getting involved again. They can also make you awfully nervous about everything that happens in a new relationship.

Which is too bad. Finding a new romance after the unhappy demise of your last relationship can be a perfectly wonderful experience.

Before we get into the problems many people encounter moving from one romance to another, it's important to keep in mind the inspiring results of finding a new boyfriend.

- You are reminded that those glorious feelings of love can happen with more than just one person. You are the one with the capacity to feel them. You own them. They are yours to give and take away.

- You are reminded that you can inspire all sorts of fabulous feelings in another person. That even though one person may have decided it was time to move on, there are other people for whom you will seem the perfect match.

- You can give yourself the opportunity to use what you've learned from each past romance and apply it to the one you have now. Rather than allowing past experiences to scare you, they can help you understand others better and find constructive ways to handle romantic problems and avoid behaviors that could create unnecessary difficulties in a relationship. As a result each new romance will feel stronger and more successful.

It's important to keep all of this in mind because it's all too easy to break up and then just "close up shop"—which means avoiding boys all together, getting involved but running at the first sign of trouble, or getting involved, but only in the most superficial way.

This is not fair to either of you.

EVERY NEW RELATIONSHIP DESERVES
A FRESH CHANCE

It's difficult to set the bad stuff from the past aside, take the good with you, and walk into the future. Sadness and hurt can haunt your every move. But it's important to be ever aware of the way in which you are carrying your past romantic problems in your back pocket. This is because if you allow them to unconsciously influence you, all kinds of problems in your new relationship will surface.

What follows is a look at the classic issues you might bring to your next relationship and how to keep them under control so that you don't unintentionally botch things up!

- ♦ You might start seeing "signs" of a breakup that aren't signs at all. Whether or not you saw your last break-up coming, you might find yourself extremely wary about every "move he makes." If he raises his voice, arches his eyebrows, has to suddenly cancel a date, acts distracted during a conversation, or fails to notice your new haircut, you might find yourself feeling very suspicious. Insecure. Afraid. But try and keep these reactions under control. No one can act completely devoted every second. And just because your boyfriend gets a little uptight over something you say, or has to cancel a date, or doesn't notice a new blouse, haircut, or jacket, doesn't mean the relationship is on the way out. It just means you're in a relationship. One in which not everyone can be "on" or available all the time.

The main thing you need to learn is how to stop reading something into everything. Use positive self-talk. When he doesn't seem attentive, remind yourself you are not the only thing in his life. He may like you a lot but be upset about something that happened at school, or at home, or with a friend, and perhaps hasn't decided to talk about it yet. If he has to cancel a date, it may actually be for the reasons he gave you! His out-of-town cousins could really be in. He might have just been handed tickets to a big ball game. The point is think to yourself, "He likes me. I'm worth it. If this keeps happening maybe I'll think twice. But right now I believe him and it will only cause tension if I start acting suspicious for no good reason."

➤ You might still be glorifying a past relationship that ended before you were ready, and your new boyfriend just can't measure up. When someone breaks up with you before you're ready, the tendency might be to only think about what you've lost, how wonderful it was, and how much you wish you could get it back. Frequently people forget all the bad stuff and remember only the good. It's difficult to look back under stressful circumstances with any clarity. It is common to hold this ex up as the "perfect boyfriend" against whom no one could compare.

You wouldn't do this on purpose of course. Still, every difference between the old and the new boyfriend may irk. Even if the new boyfriend has better traits! If he's nicer you might think, "But Sam was more unpredictable. More interesting." If he's very smart you might think, "But Andy was so athletic and smart enough." This is no way to go. Comparing will only leave you with one foot in the old relationship and one in the new. Which means you are nowhere.

You've got to stop glorifying your ex. Refer to the list of his flaws you've probably already drawn up after reading other chapters in this book. Then enlist the help of others. Talk to your friends, telling them not to hold back. What do they find unattractive about him? What do they find attractive about your new boyfriend? You need objective views, to overcome your own tunnel vision.

♦ You might decide to break up with him the moment things get rough, so you don't have to endure him breaking up with you. Once you've been hurt, you might understandably become overly defensive. Any sign that you are causing your boyfriend displeasure could inspire you to quickly say, "You know, this just doesn't feel right. I think we should end this now." But what if you've misunderstood the moment? What if it's nothing you've done, but rather his terrible mood? A problem he is tense about that has nothing to do with you? Then what you've done is passed up an opportunity to help your boyfriend hurt less, and grow closer to you. . . .

The best way to keep from running when things get rough is to talk first. But try not to express your thoughts or fears immediately. Anyone in a relationship needs to know their partner can tolerate a sour moment, a sharp word, or a dull time without feeling as if the romance is falling apart. Your boyfriend won't want to reassure you every moment. It's a turn-off. As stated earlier, no one can be on all the time. He also needs to feel that affections won't diminish at the first unpleasantness. So, the next time there's an unhappy note allow for it. Tell yourself, "This happens in all relationships." Remind yourself of the tense moments you've had with some of your best girlfriends. And most importantly, inform yourself that you are not a feather. One bad moment shouldn't blow you away. Then, if the difficult times keep coming, still don't run. Instead, talk about it. The "it" refers to the specific tensions, not the possibility of breaking up. How you approach the talk can make all the difference. (See Chapter 5.)

"I notice we seem to freeze up with each other whenever we discuss what to do on Sundays. Why do you think that is?" This approach expresses your desire to work things out. To uncover hidden problems. It is actually a very positive move.

"We're not getting along too well. Do you think we should stop spending so much time together?" suggests you want out. That you can't or don't want to get to the bottom of a problem. That you'd rather leave than give the relationship serious attention. You can't get much more negative than that. And you can bet in very short order you'll be traveling solo.

❥ You might put off a lot of boys for fear of getting involved and getting hurt again. Hiding when one is scared of something is a common reaction. You may figure if you keep everyone away, they can't hurt you. Well, that may be true. But in doing so you will hurt yourself. You will lose out in feeling close to someone. You will lose out in enjoying a romance. But most of all you will lose out in discovering that every romance is different and that you can grow and learn from each one and that they don't all end the same, and that no matter what happens you can survive!

Give boys a chance. Don't be prejudiced! Grouping them all together, thinking they're all dishonest or insensitive is as unfair as any religious or racial bigotry. Each boy deserves to be seen as an individual. Everyone is different and everyone changes a little as a result of each new involvement. A boy who might have a reputation for being insensitive or disloyal may benefit from his mistakes and make the next girl a great boyfriend! You too are different in every relationship.

You're wiser and more experienced. This can only impact positively on your future involvements. So the next time you meet someone cute and new tell yourself:

- This is a whole new person to get to know!
- I'm sure he's got problems but they can't possibly be the same as my ex's.
- I have learned things from my past. I'm going to do certain things a little differently.
- He's probably made his mistakes too. I could benefit from that.
- I've got to keep at this so that one day when the time is right I'll find the right guy for me and know just how to keep that relationship healthy and strong.

THE ALWAYS-DUMPED SYNDROME

Do you have a tendency to get, as you might put it, dumped? Are you always the one who is left? Have you decided not to chance it anymore? That there's something wrong with you?

Well, once again, there isn't.

But there probably is something wrong with what you're *doing*.

A girl who is always getting broken up with is usually someone who is using the following behaviors:

- Ignoring the signs that things are "off."
- Putting his needs consistently in front of her own.

- Forgetting to assess whether the relationship is making her feel good.

- Clinging tightly as soon as things get rocky.

- Having a desperate need for approval.

It's unfortunately very easy, extremely common, and terribly painful to wallow in the belief that "I'm not cut out for romance. No one will love me."

But believe it or not those thoughts are the coward's way out.

They are thoughts that keep you from facing the truth.

TRUTH ONE: You can't possibly enjoy a successful romance or yourself, if you consistently put aside who you are and what you need. You will merely be acting and you will always feel depressed and exhausted from the effort.

TRUTH TWO: Sticking up for yourself, chancing an argument, standing your ground, and asking for what you need will not make a person who likes you like you less. Quite the opposite. He will like you more. He will respect your sense of self and will feel the desire to please you just as you would like to please him. But within reason.

THE "HE'S NOT WHAT I WANTED
AFTER ALL" SYNDROME

What if you're the one who keeps breaking up with a guy? You think you're in love but then, like clockwork, shortly after gaining his attentions, you just lose interest? This doesn't make you happy but somehow the pattern continues. What's going on?

You could be unwilling to have just one boyfriend. You prefer dating and keeping things light. This is perfectly valid, but you might want to think twice about forming relationships. You'll leave a string of broken hearts behind and that is simply unkind. If you don't intend to form a deeper relationship, don't behave as if you do.

However, if moving from one boy to the next is making you unhappy or terribly confused, you do need to consider what's really going on.

- You are afraid to let someone really get to know you.

- You bolt the moment things feel funny to avoid being broken up with.

- You secretly fear that anyone who would like you might not be so good after all.

- You need to keep proving that you can get whomever you want in order to feel good about yourself.

If you are distressed over your tendency to walk away you may need to look at your motivations for starting the relationships and exactly what begins to happen inside you as things commence unraveling. It might be necessary to talk to your parents, good friends, or a counselor in order to gain some perspective on this upsetting (and very unfulfilling) pattern.

It could be a confidence problem. You may be afraid to open up to others for fear of getting hurt, and lack confidence in your ability to choose a trustworthy partner.

THE NOT–QUITE–READY–YET STATE

It takes time to get over a past romance. You will need to go through a few stages of "mourning" before you are ready to move forward with a new romance. The timetable is different for everyone and every circumstance. Some past relationships are easier to get over than others. Some people simply need to mourn less than others.

Wherever you stand on this issue, *take your time*.

Leaping into another romance before you are ready is a terrific way to assure that another break-up will soon be in the offing. If you're still feeling hurt, or confused or disenchanted with love, you will end up bringing these feelings into your new relationship. This does not make for a happy romance.

You have no choice but to let things take their course. Of course you don't have to wait until you feel 100 percent thrilled about everything to start a new relationship. Lots of times the best way to *completely* get over a past love is to find a new one.

The trick is to find the new one after you've truly let the old one go. He may still be on your mind, you may miss the relationship, but you are aware that it is over and time to experience feelings for someone else.

You'll know the moment. Suddenly one day you will find yourself noticing a number of guys that look, well, hmmmm . . .

NINE

WHAT MAKES A SUCCESSFUL RELATIONSHIP?

A successful relationship, for you, should not be defined by whether or not it lasts, but rather what it's like during the time you and your boyfriend are together.

Just because a relationship goes on forever doesn't make it a good relationship. Just because a relationship ends doesn't make it a bad one.

People, as we've already discovered, can stay together for all kinds of poor reasons. They're afraid to be alone, they need proof of being attractive to the opposite sex, they only feel important if they have a romantic partner, etc.

A successful relationship can be one that has a beginning, middle, and end. And this is true even if the end does not arrive smoothly, or with each partner feeling equally about it. In fact lots of successful relationships end unhappily. It's stressful and sad to lose something important.

In short, a break-up for you doesn't mean a relationship failed.

Only a miserable relationship does that!

Yes, it's true that later in life when people are more ready to settle down and make decisions about future partners, long-term relationships that break up, broken engagements, or even divorces are often seen as unsuccessful relationships. This is because the goal was usually one of a lifetime commitment. Since that hasn't happened, people think the relationship failed.

But in truth, even that's not completely true. Maybe a very big piece of these relationships was quite successful for a long time.

In any event, that is the piece of the relationship with which you need to concern yourself.

How do you have a successful relationship, even if a break-up is somewhat inevitable?

Here's a guide to making sure the relationship you've got is as good as it can be, while you've got it. Some of these points have been touched on throughout the book, but here they are all together for handy reference.

◆━━━━━━━━━━━━━━━━━━━━◆

HOW TO HAVE A SUCCESSFUL RELATIONSHIP

Understand that a romance can't feel great every moment. If you don't allow for some "down" time, you will be putting too much pressure on the relationship.

Cut both of you some slack. Neither of you is going to behave perfectly in this relationship. If you are too hard on him or too hard on yourself, both of you will be afraid to say or do anything.

Offer an apology when you are wrong and accept his. There's plenty of time in the future to notice if his apologies are meaningless.

Be brave and aware. This means about yourself *and* him. If you sense something is wrong with

99

the relationship, admit it to yourself. It's not going to just go away if you ignore it. But don't torture yourself or him with anxious thoughts. Just try to understand what's happening.

Think in terms of what you can give and don't keep a balance sheet to make sure you're getting it all back. Surely you've noticed a particular girlfriend is better than another at comforting you. Someone else still gives you the biggest laughs. No one can be everything to you. It's important to give what you've got (a good listening ear or an insightful way of thinking) whether or not you get it back. After all, chances are, your girlfriend gives something to you that you can't return. Well, it's the same with a boyfriend. He can't be all things for you, nor can you for him.

He can be a very important part of your life, but he shouldn't be the only important person in your life. Too much dependence on him and too little attention and respect paid to your friends will make for a lot of problems. He may not be able to stand the constant pressure and you will lose other relationships that are just as important and which can offer you things a boyfriend may not be able to.

Always be sensitive but honest. Say how you feel, always remembering that there is a vulnerable person in front of you. Everyone leaves themselves unprotected when they allow themselves an involvement with another person. They deserve straight but gentle talk: Words that speak the truth but at the same time protect their feelings as much as possible. This is true at the beginning, middle, and end of any relationship.

Break-ups are a drag. Healing time can hurt.

But what follows can bring tremendous joy. So go with the process. Don't be afraid of the sadness. It's part of the deal. It's what you have to go through.

It's the price you pay for a ticket to an even better new romance.

Dear Reader,

I hope that you've found *Help! My Heart is Breaking!* both informative and helpful, and I'd love to hear from you. Are there other topics you'd like to see books written about? Do you have a burning question that you've never seen answered anywhere? Is there something you need help with? Boys? Dating? Your parents?

Drop me a note, care of:

Avon Books
1350 Avenue of the Americas
Room 222
New York, New York 10019

Take Care.

Meg Schneider